THE NIGHT PEACOCK
(1911)

HERMANN HESSE

Domesday Books

The Night Peacock

Title: The Night Peacock Butterfly
Author: Herman Hesse
Translator: Seika
Publisher: Domesday Books
ISBN: 978-1-7325730-4-8
Norfolk Virginia USA
Copyright©2021 Domesday Books

Das Nachtpfauenauge

Mein Gast und Freund Heinrich Mohr war von seinem Abendspaziergang heimgekehrt und saß nun bei mir im Studierzimmer, noch beim letzen Tageslicht. Vor den Fenstern lag weit hinaus der bleiche See, scharf vom hügeligen Ufer gesäumt.

The Night Peacock

My guest and a friend Heinrich Mohr was back from his evening walk and was now sitting by me in the study, where there were the last, lingering remains of daylight. The faded lake lay far out in front of the window, sharply fringed by the hilly shore.

The Night Peacock

Wir sprachen, da eben mein kleiner

Sohn uns gute Nacht gesagt hatte,

von Kindern und von Kindererinnerungen.

The Night Peacock

We were talking about children and childhood memories, since my little son had just said good night to us.

»Seit ich Kinder habe«,

sagte ich,

»ist schon manche Liebhaberei

der eigenen Knabenzeit wieder

bei mir lebendig geworden. Seit

einem Jahr etwa habe ich sogar

wieder eine Schmetterlingssammlung

angefangen. Willst du sie sehen?«

"Since I have had children,"

I said,

"many of my own boyhood hobbies have come back to life. For the last year or so, I have even started a butterfly collection again. Do you want to see it?"

The Night Peacock

Er bat darum, und ich ging hinaus,

um zwei oder drei von den leichten

Pappkästen hereinzuholen. Als ich den

ersten öffnete, merkten wir beide erst,

wie dunkel es schon geworden war; man

konnte kaum noch die Umrisse der

aufgespannten Falter erkennen. Ich griff zur

Lampe und strich ein Zündholz an, und

augenblicklich versank die Landschaft

draußen, und die Fenster standen voll von

undurchdringlichem Nachtblau.

The Night Peacock

He wanted to see it, so I stepped out of my study to go and fetch two or three light cardboard boxes. When I opened the first box, we both realized for the first time how dark it had already become; one could barely make out the outlines of the butterflies that were spread out. I grabbed a lamp and struck a match, and instantly the landscape outside sank, and the windows were full of an impenetrable night blue.

Meine Schmetterlinge aber Leuchteten in dem
hellen Lampenlicht prächtig aus dem
Kasten. Wir beugten uns darüber,
betrachteten die schönfarbigen Gebilde und
nannten ihre Namen.

The Night Peacock

My butterflies, however, shone magnificently from the box in the bright lamplight. We leaned over them and looked at their beautifully colored shapes, and called their names.

»Das da ist ein gelbes Ordensband«,

sagte ich,

»lateinisch fulminea, das gilt hier für selten.«

"That is a *yellow-banded underwing,* "

I said,

"*fulminea* in Latin. It's regarded as rare here."

Heinrich Mohr hatte vorsichtig einen der
Schmetterlinge an seiner Nadel aus dem
Kasten gezogen und betrachtete die
Unterseite seiner Flügel.

The Night Peacock

Heinrich Mohr carefully took one of the butterflies out of the box at its pin and examined the inner side of its wings.

»Merkwürdig«,

sagte er,

»kein Anblick weckt die

Kindheitserinnerungen so stark in mir

wie der von Schmetterlingen.«

"Remarkable,"

he said,

"nothing awakens childhood memories in me

as powerfully as the sight of butterflies."

Und, indem er den Falter wieder an

seinem Ort ansteckte und den Kastendeckel

schloß: »Genug davon! «

And as he pinned the butterfly back in its place and closed the lid of the box.

"Enough of that!"

Er sagte es hart und rasch, als wären diese Erinnerungen ihm unlieb.

He said that harshly and abruptly, as if he hated those memories.

Gleich darauf, da ich den Kasten
weggetragen hatte und wieder hereinkam,
lächelte er mit seinem braunen, schmalen
Gesicht und bat um eine Zigarette.

Right after that, as I had carried the box away and came back in, he smiled with his narrow, tanned face and asked for a cigarette.

»Du mußt mir's nicht übelnehmen«,

sagte er dann,

»wenn ich deine Sammlung nicht

genauer angeschaut habe.

"You mustn't take it amiss that I did not
have a proper look at your collection,"
he said.

Ich habe als Junge natürlich auch eine gehabt,
aber leider habe ich mir selber die Erinnerung
daran verdorben. Ich kann es dir ja erzählen,
obwohl es eigentlich schmählich ist. «

I also had a collection when I was a boy, of course. But sadly, I ruined my memory of it. I can tell you the story, even though it is quite disgraceful."

Er zündete seine Zigarette über dem

Lampenzylinder an, setzte den grünen

Schirm über die Lampe, so daß unsre Gesichter

in Dämmerung sanken,

He lit his cigarette over the lamp cylinder, and put the green shade over the lamp. Our faces sank into dusk.

und setzte sich auf das Gesims des offenen Fensters, wo seine schlanke hagere Figur sich kaum von der Finsternis abhob.

The Night Peacock

He sat on a cornice* of the open window,

where his slim, gaunt figure barely stood out

from the darkness.

<* a horizontal architectural element of a building,
projecting forward from the main walls, originally
used as a means of directing rainwater away from the
building's walls. Hesse probably meant 'window
sill'>

The Night Peacock

Und während ich eine Zigarette rauchte und draußen das hochtönige ferne Singen der Frösche die Nacht erfüllte, erzählte mein Freund das Folgende.

The Night Peacock

And while I smoked a cigarette and outside the frogs' high-pitched distant singing filled the night, my friend told me the following.

Das Schmetterlingssammeln fing ich mit

acht oder neun Jahren an und trieb es anfangs

ohne besonderen Eifer wie andre Spiele und

Liebhabereien auch.

The Night Peacock

I started collecting butterflies when I was eight or nine years old. At first, I did it without any passion, like other games and hobbies.

Aber im zweiten Sommer, als ich etwa zehn
Jahre alt war, da nahm dieser Sport mich ganz
gefangen

But in the second summer, when I was about ten years old, this sport captivated me completely.

und wurde zu einer solchen Leidenschaft, daß man ihn mir mehrmals meinte verbieten zu müssen, da ich alles darüber vergaß und versäumte.

The Night Peacock

It became such a passion that people
repeatedly thought of forbidding me from
doing it because I forgot and neglected
everything because of it.

War ich auf Falterfang, dann hörte ich keine
Turmuhr schlagen, sei es zur Schule oder
zum Mittagessen,

If I was catching butterflies, I didn't hear any tower clock striking, whether it was time for school or lunch.

und in den Ferien war ich oft, mit einem

Stück Brot in der Botanisierbüchse,

vom frühen Morgen bis zur Nacht draußen,

ohne zu einer Mahlzeit heimzukommen.

The Night Peacock

And during the holidays, I was often outdoors
with a piece of bread in the botanizer's box
from early morning to night without coming
home for a meal.

Ich spüre etwas von dieser Leidenschaft
noch jetzt manchmal, wenn ich besonders
schöne Schmetterlinge sehe.

The Night Peacock

Sometimes, when I see a particularly beautiful butterfly, I still feel a trace of that passion.

The Night Peacock

Dann überfällt mich für Augenblicke

wieder das namenlose, gierige Entzücken,

das nur Kinder empfinden können, und mit

dem ich als Knabe meinen ersten

Schwalbenschwanz beschlich.

The Night Peacock

Then for a moment, I am overcome by the nameless, devouring ecstasy that only children can feel. That feeling with which I crept my first swallowtail as a boy.

Und dann fallen mir plötzlich ungezählte

Augenblicke und Stunden der Kinderzeitein,

glühende Nachmittage in der trockenen, stark

duftenden Heide,

And then suddenly I remember the countless
moments and hours of childhood, glowing
afternoons in the dry, strong-scented
heathland,

The Night Peacock

kühle Morgenstunden im Garten oder

Abende an geheimnisvollen Waldrändern,

wo ich mit meinem Netz auf der Lauer stand

wie ein Schatzsucher und jeden Augenblick

auf die tollsten Überraschungen und

Beglückungen gefaßt war.

The Night Peacock

cool mornings in the garden or evenings at the

mysterious edges of the forest, where I stood

waiting with my net like a treasure hunter,

ready for the most amazing surprises

and delights at any moment.

The Night Peacock

Und wenn ich dann einen schönen Falter
sah, er brauchte nicht einmal besonders selten
zu sein, wenn er auf einem Blumenstengel in
der Sonne saß und die farbigen Flügel atmend
auf und ab bewegte und mir die Jagdlust den
Atem verschlug,

The Night Peacock

And when I saw a beautiful butterfly or moth –
it didn't even have to be particularly rare-
when it was sitting on a flower stem in the sun
and move its colourful wings up and down
breathing, the desire for hunting took my
breath away.

wenn ich näher und näher schlich und jeden

leuchtenden Farbenfleck und jede kristallene

Flügelader und jedes feine braune Haar der

Fühler sehen konnte,

The Night Peacock

When I crept closer and closer and could see
the spot of bright colours and every crystal
wing vein and every fine brown down of
the antennae,

The Night Peacock

das war eine Spannung und Wonne, eine
Mischung von zarter Freude mit wilder
Begierde, die ich später im Leben selten
mehr empfunden habe.

that was a thrill and delight, a mixture of
tender joy with wild desire… something I
seldom felt later in life.

Meine Sammlung mußte ich, da meine Eltern arm waren und mir nichts dergleichen schenken konnten, in einer gewöhnlichen alten Kartonschachtel aufbewahren.

The Night Peacock

Since my parents were poor and couldn't give me anything of the kind, I had to keep my collection in an ordinary old cardboard box.

The Night Peacock

Ich klebte runde Korkscheiben, aus
Flaschenpfropfen geschnitten, auf den Boden,
um die Nadeln darein zu stecken, und
zwischen den zerknickten Pappdeckelwänden
dieser Schachtel hegte ich meine Schätze.

The Night Peacock

I glued round cork discs cut from bottle
stoppers on the bottom to put the needles in,
and I kept my treasures between the crumpled
cardboard walls of this box.

The Night Peacock

Anfangs zeigte ich gern und häufig meine

Sammlung den Kameraden, aber andere hatten

Holzkästen mit Glasdekkeln,

Raupenschachteln mit grünen Gazewänden

und anderen Luxus, so daß ich mit meiner

primitiven Einrichtung mich nicht eben

brüsten konnte.

The Night Peacock

At first, I liked showing my collection to my
mates frequently, but they had wooden cases
with glass covers, crawler boxes with
green gauze walls, and other luxuries, so I
couldn't brag about my primitive equipment.

The Night Peacock

Auch war mein Bedürfnis danach nicht groß und ich gewöhnte mir an, sogar wichtige und ufregende Fänge zu verschweigen und die Beute nur meinen Schwestern zu zeigen.

The Night Peacock

After that, my desire was not great either, and even for the important and exciting loot, I got used to concealing them and showed my loot only to my sisters.

The Night Peacock

Einmal hatte ich den bei uns seltenen blauen
Schillerfalter erbeutet und aufgespannt, und
als er trokken war, trieb mich der Stolz, ihn
doch wenigstens meinem Nachbarn zu zeigen,
dem Sohn eines Lehrers, der überm Hof
wohnte.

The Night Peacock

One day, I captured a *blue emperor* which is rare
here. I spread its wings, and when it dried, my
pride drove me at least to show it to my
neighbour, a teacher's son who lived across
the courtyard.

The Night Peacock

Dieser Junge hatte das Laster der
Tadellosigkeit, das bei Kindern doppelt
unheimlich ist. Er besaß eine kleine
unbedeutende Sammlung, die aber durch ihre
Nettigkeit und exakte Erhaltung zu einem
Juwel wurde.

The Night Peacock

This boy had the vice of faultlessness,

which is doubly incredible in children.

Children found him exceptionally uncanny.

He had a small, insignificant collection,

but due to its attractiveness and the exact

preservation made it a gem.

Er verstand sogar die seltene und
schwierige Kunst, beschädigte und
zerbrochene Falterflügel wieder
zusammenzuleimen, und war in jeder
Hinsicht ein Musterknabe, weshalb ich
ihn denn mit Neid und halber
Bewunderung haßte.

The Night Peacock

He was versed even in the rare

and challenging skill of gluing

the damaged and broken butterfly

wings together, and was a model boy

in every respect-which is why

I hated him with envy

and half-admiration.

Diesem jungen Idealknaben zeigte ich
meinen Schillerfalter. Er begutachtete ihn
fachmännisch, anerkannte seine Seltenheit
und sprach ihm einen Barwert von etwa
zwanzig Pfennigen zu; denn der Knabe
Emil wußte alle Sammelobjekte, zumal
Briefmarken und Schmetterlinge, nach
ihrem Geldwert zu taxieren.

The Night Peacock

I showed my *purple-blue emperor* to this ideal
young boy. He examined it expertly,
recognized its rarity and gave it a value of
about twenty pfennigs because this boy Emil
knew how to assign monetary value to all
collectibles, especially postage stamps and
butterflies, according to their monetary value.

Dann fing er aber an zu ritisieren, fand
meinen Blauschiller schlecht aufgespannt,
den rechten Fühler gebogen, den linken
ausgestreckt, und entdeckte richtig auch
noch einen Defekt, denn dem Falter
fehlten zwei Beine.

The Night Peacock

But then he began to criticize, finding my
blue emperor badly stretched, the right antenna
bent, the left one outstretched, and he also
correctly discovered another defect, namely,
that the butterfly was missing two legs.

The Night Peacock

Ich schlug zwar diesen Mangel nicht hoch
an, doch hatte mir der Nörgler die Freude
an meinem Schiller einigermaßen
verdorben und ich habe ihm nie mehr
meine Beute gezeigt.

The Night Peacock

I hadn't thought much about such defects, but the nitpicker had ruined my pleasure for my butterfly to some extent, and I never showed him my catch again.

Zwei Jahre später, wir waren schon große Buben, aber meine Leidenschaft war noch in voller Blüte, verbreitete sich das Gerücht, jener Emil habe ein Nachtpfauenauge gefangen.

The Night Peacock

Two years later, we had grown into big boys, but my passion was still in full bloom. The rumour spread that Emil had caught a *night peacock*.

Das war nun für mich weit aufregender
als wenn ich heute höre, daß ein Freund
von mir eine Million geerbt oder die
verlorenen Bücher des Livius gefunden
habe.

The Night Peacock

The news was far more exciting for me than when I hear today that a friend of mine has inherited a million or found the lost books of Livy.

The Night Peacock

Das Nachtpfauenauge hatte noch keiner
von uns gefangen, ich kannte es überhaupt
nur aus der Abbildung eines alten
Schmetterlingsbuches, das ich besaß und
dessen mit der Hand olorierte Kupfer
unendlich viel schöner und eigentlich auch
exakter waren als alle modernen
Farbendrucke.

The Night Peacock

None of us had caught a *night peacock*, I knew it
only from the illustration in an old butterfly
book that I had, and its hand-coloured
copperplates infinitely more beautiful and far
more precise than all modern colour prints.

Von allen Schmetterlingen, deren Namen
ich kannte und die in meiner Schachtel
noch fehlten, ersehnte ich keinen so
glühend wie das Nachtpfauenauge.

The Night Peacock

Of all the butterflies whose names I knew, and were still missing from my box, I longed for nothing as passionately as for the *night peacock*.

Oft hatte ich die Abbildung in meinem
Buch betrachtet, und ein Kamerad hatte
mir erzählt: Wenn der braune Falter an
einem Baumstamm oder Felsen sitze und
ein Vogel oder anderer Feind ihn angreifen
wolle, so ziehe er nur die gefalteten
dunkleren Vorderflügel auseinander und
zeige die schönen Hinterflügel, deren große
helle Augen so erkwürdig und unerwartet
aussähen, daß der Vogel erschrecke und den
Schmetterling in Ruhe lasse.

The Night Peacock

I had often looked at the illustration in my book. A mate would tell me: When the brown butterfly is sitting on a tree trunk or a rock, and a bird or other enemies want to attack it, it raises the folded darker forewings up to show its beautiful hindwings. Its big, bright eyes look so strange and unexpected that the bird would be frightened and leaves the butterfly alone.

Dieses Wundertier sollte der langweilige Emil haben! Als ich es hörte, empfand ich im ersten Augenblick nur die Freude, endlich das seltene Tier zu Gesicht zu bekommen und eine brennende Neugierde darauf.

The Night Peacock

And to think that boring Emil should have this miraculous animal! When I heard about it, I just felt the joy to finally get to see the rare animal, and a burning curiosity.

Dann stellte sich freilich der Neid
ein, und es schien mir schnöde zu
sein, daß gerade dieser Langweiler und
Mops den geheimnisvollen kostbaren
Falter hatte erwischen müssen. Darum
bezwang ich mich auch und tat ihm die
Ehre nicht an, hinüberzugehen und mir
seinen Fang zeigen zu lassen.

The Night Peacock

Then, of course, jealousy set in, and it seemed despicable to me that it should be precisely this bore and pug who had caught the mysterious, precious butterfly. So, I controlled myself too and did not give him the honour to go over to his place to let him show me his catch.

Doch brachte ich meine edanken von der Sache nicht los, und am nächsten Tage, als das Gerücht sich in der Schule bestätigte, war ich sofort entschlossen, doch hinzugehen.

The Night Peacock

Still, I couldn't get it off my mind. And the next
day, when the rumor was confirmed at school,
I decided to go there right away.

Nach Tisch, sobald ich vom Hause
wegkonnte, lief ich über den Hof und in
den dritten Stock des Nachbarhauses
hinauf, wo neben Mägdekammern und
Holzverschlägen der Lehrerssohn ein oft
von mir beneidetes kleines Stübchen für
sich allein ewohnen durfte.

The Night Peacock

After dinner, as soon as I was allowed to leave the house, I ran across the courtyard and up to the third floor of the neighboring house, where in addition to maids' rooms and wooden crates, the teacher's son had a small room that I often envied.

Niemand begegnete mir unterwegs, und als
ich oben an die Kammertür klopfte, erhielt
ich keine Antwort. Emil war nicht da, und
als ich die Türklinke versuchte, fand ich den
Eingang offen, den er sonst während
seiner Abwesenheit peinlich verschloß.

The Night Peacock

I saw no one on the way, and when I knocked
on the door upstairs, I received no answer.
Emil wasn't there. When I tried the doorknob, I
found the entrance open, which he usually
meticulously locked when he was away.

The Night Peacock

Ich trat ein, um das Tier doch wenigstens
zu sehen, und nahm sofort die beiden
großen Schachteln vor, in welchen Emil
seine Sammlung verwahrte. In beiden
suchte ich vergebens, bis mir einfiel, der
Falter werde noch auf dem Spannbrett sein.

I stepped in to at least see the animal and immediately took the two large boxes from in which Emil kept his collection. I searched through both in vain, until it occurred to me that the butterfly would still be on the setting block.

The Night Peacock

Da fand ich ihn denn auch: die braunen
Flügel mit schmalen Papierstreifen
überspannt, hing das Nachtpfauenauge
am Brett, ich beugte mich darüber und
sah alles aus nächster Nähe an, die
behaarten hellbraunen Fühler, die
eleganten und unendlich zart gefärbten
Flügelränder, die feine wollige Behaarung
am Innenrand der unteren Flügel.

The Night Peacock

There I found it. Its brown wings stretched out
with narrow paper strips, the *night peacock*
was hung on the board. I leaned over it and
looked closely at everything: the downy, light
brown antennae, the elegant and extremely
delicately coloured wing edges, the fine woolly
down on the inner edge of the lower wings.

Nur gerade die Augen konnte ich nicht sehen, die waren vom Papierstreifen verdeckt.

Mit Herzklopfen gab ich der Versuchung nach, die Streifen loszumachen, und zog die Stecknadel heraus.

However, I couldn't see its eyes. They were covered by the paper strip.

My heart pounding, I gave in to the temptation to untie the strips, and I pulled out the pin.

Da sahen mich die vier großen

merkwürdigen Augen an, weit schöner

und wunderlicher als auf der Abbildung,

Then the four big, extraordinary eyes looked at me, far more beautiful and wondrous than on pictures.

und bei ihrem Anblick fühlte ich eine

so unwiderstehliche Begierde nach dem

Besitz des herrlichen Tieres, daß ich

unbedenklich den ersten Diebstahl

meines Lebens beging, indem ich sachte an

der Nadel zog und den Schmetterling, der

schon trocken war und die Form nicht verlor,

in der hohlen Hand aus der Kammer trug.

At the sight of it, I felt such an overwhelming desire to own the beautiful animal, that I committed the first theft of my life- harmlessly- by gently pulling the needle and carrying the butterfly, which was already dry and had not lost its shape, out of the chamber in my cupped hand.

Dabei hatte ich kein Gefühl als das einer

ungeheuren Befriedigung.

In doing so, I felt nothing except an immense satisfaction.

Das Tier in der rechten Hand verborgen,

ging ich die Treppe hinab.

The Night Peacock

Hiding the butterfly in my right hand, I went

down the stairs.

Da hörte ich, daß von unten mir jemand
entgegenkam, und in dieser Sekunde
wurde mein Gewissen wach, ich wußte
plötzlich, daß ich gestohlen hatte und ein
gemeiner Kerl war;

The Night Peacock

Then I heard someone coming towards me from below, and in that second my conscience woke up, I suddenly knew that I had stolen and that I was a bad guy.

zugleich befiel mich eine ganz schreckliche

Angst vor der Entdeckung, so daß ich

instinktiv die Hand, die den Raub

umschlossen hielt, in die Tasche meiner

Jacke steckte.

The Night Peacock

At the same time, a terrible fear of being discovered came over me, so that I put the hand that held the loot instinctively in the pocket of my jacket.

Langsam ging ich weiter, zitternd und
mit einem kalten Gefühl von
Verworfenheit und Schande, ging
angstvoll an dem heraufkommenden
Dienstmädchen vorbei und blieb an der
Haustüre stehen, mit klopfendem Herzen
und schwitzender Stirn, fassungslos und vor
mir selbst erschrocken.

The Night Peacock

Slowly I walked on, trembling and with a cold feeling of depravity and disgrace. I walked fearfully past the coming maid and stopped at the front door, heart pounding and forehead sweating, stunned and terrified of myself.

Alsbald wurde mir klar, daß ich den Falter
nicht behalten könne und dürfe, daß ich
ihn zurücktragen und alles nach
Möglichkeit ungeschehen machen müsse. So
kehrte ich denn, trotz aller Angst vor einer
Begegnung und Entdeckung, schnell wieder
um, sprang mit Eile die Stiege hinan und
stand eine Minute später wieder in Emils
Kammer.

Immediately I realized that I could not and should not keep the butterfly, and that I had to carry it back and undo everything if possible. So, braving all fear of an encounter and discovery, I quickly turned around, ran up the stairs with haste, and a minute later I was back in Emil's room.

The Night Peacock

Vorsichtig zog ich die Hand aus der
Tasche und legte den Schmetterling auf
den Tisch, und ehe ich ihn wieder sah,
wußte ich das Unglück schon und war
dem Weinen nah, denn das
Nachtpfauenauge war zerstört.

The Night Peacock

Carefully I pulled my hand out of my pocket and put the butterfly on the table. Before I saw it again, I already knew that disaster had happened and was close to crying because the *night peacock* was destroyed.

Es fehlte der rechte Vorderflügel und der rechte Fühler, und als ich den abgebrochenen Flügel vorsichtig aus der Tasche zu ziehen suchte, war er zerschlissen und an kein Flicken mehr zu denken.

The Night Peacock

The right forewing and the right antennae
were missing and when I tried to carefully pull
the broken wing out of my pocket, it was torn
to shreds, and there was no longer any thought
of mending it.

Beinahe noch mehr als das Gefühl des Diebstahls peinigte mich nun der Anblick des schönen seltenen Tieres, das ich zerstört hatte.

The Night Peacock

Almost more than the feeling of theft, I was now more tormented by the sight of the beautiful, rare animal that I had destroyed.

The Night Peacock

Ich sah an meinen Fingern den zarten
braunen Flügelstaub hängen und den
zerrissenen Flügel daliegen, und hätte
jeden Besitz und jede Freude gern
 hingegeben, um ihn wieder ganz zu
wissen.

The Night Peacock

I saw the delicate brown wing dust on my fingers and the torn wing lying there. I would have gladly given up every possession and every joy to know it was whole again.

Traurig ging ich nach Hause und saß den ganzen Nachmittag in unsrem kleinen Garten, bis ich in der Dämmerung den Mut fand, meiner Mutter alles zu erzählen. Ich merkte wohl, wie sie erschrak und traurig wurde, aber sie mochte fühlen, daß schon dies Geständnis mich mehr gekostet habe als die Erduldung jeder Strafe.

The Night Peacock

I went home feeling sad and sat in our little garden all afternoon until dusk when I found the courage to tell my mother everything. I noticed how shocked and sad she was, but maybe she felt this confession made me feel worse than the enduring any punishment.

»Du mußt zum Emil hinübergehen«,

sagte sie bestimmt,

»und es ihm selber sagen. Das ist das

einzige, was du tun kannst, und ehe das

nicht geschehen ist, kann ich dir nicht

verzeihen. Du kannst ihm anbieten, daß er

sich irgendetwas von deinen Sachen

aussucht, als Ersatz, und du mußt ihn

bitten, daß er dir verzeiht.«

"You must go over to Emil's,"

she said firmly,

"and tell him yourself. It's the only thing you

can do, and until you do that, I can't forgive

you. You can offer him to choose something

you have as a replacement, and you must ask

him to forgive you. "

The Night Peacock

Das wäre mir nun bei jedem anderen Kameraden leichter gefallen als bei dem Musterknaben. Ich fühlte im voraus genau, daß er mich nicht verstehen und mir womöglich gar nicht glauben würde, und es wurde Abend und beinahe Nacht, ohne daß ich hinzugehen vermochte.

The Night Peacock

That would have been much easier for me with any other mates than with the model boy. I felt that he wouldn't understand me and probably wouldn't believe me at all, and it was evening and almost night while I couldn't go there.

Da fand mich meine Mutter unten im
Hausgang und sagte leise: »Es muß heut
noch sein, geh jetzt!«

Then my mother found me downstairs in the
doorway and said softly:

"It must be today. Go now!"

The Night Peacock

Und da ging ich hinüber und fragte im
untern Stock nach Emil, er kam und
erzählte sofort, es habe ihm jemand das
Nachtpfauenauge kaputt gemacht, er
wisse nicht, ob ein schlechter Kerl oder
vielleicht ein Vogel oder die Katze, und ich
bat ihn, mit mir hinaufzugehen und es mir
zu zeigen.

The Night Peacock

And then I went over and asked for Emil on the lower floor. He came and immediately told me that someone had destroyed his *night peacock*. He didn't know whether it was a bad guy or maybe a bird or a cat. I asked him to go up with me and show it to me.

The Night Peacock

Wir gingen hinauf, er schloß die
Kammertür auf und zündete eine Kerze
an, und ich sah auf dem Spannbrett den
verdorbenen Falter liegen.

We went upstairs. He unlocked the door and lit a candle. And I saw the damaged butterfly lying on the tensioning board.

Ich sah, daß er daran gearbeitet hatte, ihn
wieder herzustellen, der kaputte Flügel
war sorgfältig ausgebreitet und auf ein
feuchtes Fließpapier gelegt, aber er war
unheilbar, und der Fühler fehlte ja auch.
Nun sagte ich, daß ich es gewesen sei,
und versuchte zu erzählen und zu
erklären.

I saw that he had worked to restore it. The broken wing was carefully spread out and placed on damp blotting paper, but it was irreparable. And the feeler was also missing. Then I said it was me who did it and tried to explain.

Da pfiff Emil, statt wild zu werden und

mich anzuschreien, leise durch die Zähne,

sah mich eine ganze Weile still an und

sagte dann:

»So so, also so einer bist du.«

Then Emil, instead of becoming furious and screaming at me, softly whistled through his teeth. He looked at me quietly for a while and then said:

"So, so, that's how you are."

Ich bot ihm alle meine Spielsachen an, und
als er kühl blieb und mich immer noch
verächtlich ansah, bot ich ihm meine ganze
Schmetterlingssammlung an. Er sagte aber:
»Danke schön, ich kenne deine Sammlung
schon. Man hat ja heut wieder sehen
können, wie du mit Schmetterlingen
umgehst.«
In diesem Augenblicke fehlte nicht viel,
so wäre ich ihm an die Gurgel
gesprungen.

The Night Peacock

I offered him all my toys, and when he
remained cold and still looking at me with
contempt, I offered him my entire collection of
butterflies. But he said,
"Thank you. I already know your collection.
I could see how you treat butterflies again
today. "
At that moment, I came close to jumping at his
throat.

The Night Peacock

Es war nichts zu machen, ich war und blieb

ein Schuft, und Emil stand kühl in

verächtlicher Gerechtigkeit vor mir wie

die Weltordnung. Er schimpfte nicht einmal,

er sah mich nur an und verachtete mich

Nothing could be done. I was a scoundrel, and I remained a scoundrel. And Emil stood cold in contemptuous righteousness before me like the World Order. He didn't even get angry. He just stared at me and despised me.

Da sah ich zum erstenmal, daß man nichts wieder gut machen kann, was einmal verdorben ist.

The Night Peacock

For the first time, I saw that nothing could
be done to mend something once it is ruined.

Ich ging weg und war froh, daß die
Mutter mich nicht ausfragte, sondern mir
einen Kuß gab und mich in Ruhe ließ. Ich
sollte zu Bett gehen, es war schon spät für
mich. Vorher aber holte ich heimlich im
Eßzimmer die große braune Schachtel,
stellte sie aufs Bett und machte sie im
Dunkeln auf.

The Night Peacock

I went away. I was glad that my mother didn't
ask me questions but gave me a kiss and left
me alone. I should go to bed; it was already
late for me. But first I secretly fetched a big
brown box from the dining room. I placed it on
my bed and opened it in the dark.

The Night Peacock

Und dann nahm ich die Schmetterlinge
heraus, einen nach dem andern,
und drückte sie mit den Fingern zu Staub
und Fetzen.

The Night Peacock

And then, I took out the butterflies, one by one, and pressed them with my fingers to dust and shreds.

The Night Peacock

The Night Peacock

About the story

The Night Peacock was written by Hermann Hesse in 1911. He later rewrote it in 1931 and changed its title to *Jugendgedenken* (memory of youth), which was featured in a local German newspapers *The Würzburger General-Anzeiger*. This story has been used in many middle school textbooks in Japan since 1927. Almost every Japanese read this in Japanese class (as a part of translated/foreign literature). But sadly, it's not very well known in other countries.

The story begins with the writer's narration, where his guest and friend had come back from his evening walk and sat by him, and the writer's youngest child came to say good night. The child went to bed, and now time to relax and enjoy adult time. They talked about their children and their childhood memories. The writer (the first narrator I) tells his friend that he started collecting butterflies again and shows him his collection. (Note: In Germany, butterflies and moths are regarded as the same.) They realize for the first time how dark it has become, and the writer lights the light. It shines on the butterflies, and the scene outside the window suddenly sinks into the darkness, separating the outside world and the butterflies; it creates the atmosphere of remembering the past. The visitor looks at it briefly but soon closes the box, saying that's enough. He apologizes for not looking at the collection well. He says he also passionately collected butterflies as a child but ended up ruining the memory. He decides to talk about his shameful memory. He lights a cigarette with the lamp fire, puts a green shade over it; the room gets darker. He sits at the window. It is hard to see his face.   The friend in the dark can no longer be seen. Then the narrator changes from the author to the guest and friend, Heinrich Mohr throughout the rest of the book, talking of the dark past.

Heinrich Mohr began collecting butterflies when I was about 8 or 9. He wasn't all that serious at first, but he was captivated by it in the second summer, and nothing could stop him though people tried to stop me many times. He did not care if it was time for school or a meal. He was completely obsessed by it, feeling overcome by the nameless, devouring ecstasy that only children can feel. His parents were poor and did not give him proper tools. So he made his own had to make his own using an old cardboard box, and didn't show his collection to his friends because all other friends had proper ones. But when he caught a rare butterfly, he showed it to Emil, a teacher's son who lived across the courtyard. Emil was impeccability vice, and children found him exceptionally uncanny. He even had the rare and challenging skill to glue damaged and torn butterfly wings together. He was a model boy in every respect. Heinrich Mohr hated Emil with envy and half admiration. At first, Emil admitted the rareness of the butterfly and even estimated its value. Then he began to find many defects. After that, he never showed him his catch again.

Two years later, when his desire for butterflies was at its prime, he heard a rumour that Emil had caught a night-peacock butterfly. No one around him had caught one before. He only knew it only from the illustration of an old butterfly book. He was overexcited and went to his place. Emil was not there but the door was unlocked. He could not control his desire to see the butterfly and went into the room and found the butterfly on a setting block. Captivated by the butterfly's beauty, he removed the butterfly and left the room with it, feeling nothing except the immense satisfaction. But suddenly he heard someone coming up the stairs and he put the hand holding the butterfly into his pocket. He realises what he did was wrong and quickly turned around, hurried up the stairs and a minute later stood in Emil's room to return it. But when he took it out of his pocket, he found the butterfly was destroyed and unrepairable.

He went home feeling guilty and told his mother everything. She told him he must go over to Emil and tell him and offer him to choose something he has as a replacement and ask him to forgive him. He went to Emil's room and told him. Instead of getting angry, Emil remained calm. He said, 'So, that's what you are,' refusing to accept his collection of butterflies as a replacement and said, "I already know your collection. Besides, I could see how you treat butterflies again today."

After he went home, he secretly fetched a big brown box from the dining room, placed it on his bed and opened it in the dark, took out the butterflies, one by one, and pressed them with his fingers to dust and shreds. Maybe the strong inferiority complex, defeat, regret, and resentment for Emil has peaked. Maybe by doing so, he was punishing himself or perhaps putting an end to his innocent childhood by destroying his butterflies with his own hands.

Hermann Karl Hesse

Hermann Hesse (born July 2, 1877, Calw, Germany — died August 9, 1962, Montagnola, Switzerland) is a German novelist and poet who was awarded the Nobel Prize for Literature in 1946.

About the translator

English-Japanese freelance translator. Graduate of Fukuoka University in Fukuoka Japan. Bachelor of Arts in German studies.

Many thanks to:

Ms Tara Moller of **DreamPunk Press** and **Vesna V. Bukilica** for their help♥♥♥

The Night Peacock